This Winnie-the-Pooh
book belongs to:

..................................................

# EGMONT

*We bring stories to life*

First Published in Great Britain 2011
This edition published in 2015
by Egmont UK Limited
The Yellow Building, 1 Nicholas Road, London W11 4AN

Illustrated by Andrew Grey
Copyright © 2015 Disney Enterprises, Inc.
Based on the "Winnie the Pooh" works,
by A.A.Milne and E.H.Shepard

ISBN 978 1 4052 7940 6
48547/009
Printed in UK

# Winnie-the-Pooh
# Pooh's Snowy Day

**EGMONT**

One morning Pooh wasn't doing very much, so he thought he would go and visit Piglet. But when he got to Piglet's house, Piglet wasn't there. Bother, thought Pooh to himself, and he decided to go back home.

When Pooh got back to his own house, he found Piglet sitting in his best armchair. For a moment he wondered whose house he was in.

"Hello Piglet," he said. "I thought you were out."

"No," said Piglet. "It's you who were out, Pooh!"

When they had had a little something to eat, Pooh and Piglet decided to visit Eeyore. On the way they sang a special outdoor song that Pooh had written:

"*The more it snows, Tiddley Pom!*" it went.

By this time Pooh and Piglet were close to where Eeyore lived.

"I've been thinking," said Pooh. "Eeyore's place is very gloomy. Why don't we build him a new house?"

"I saw a heap of sticks on the other side of the wood," said Piglet, helpfully.

"Let's go and fetch them," said Pooh, "and build a house here."

A little bit later, Christopher Robin was just about to go outside when who should arrive at his front door but Eeyore.

"Hello Christopher Robin," said Eeyore. "I don't suppose you've seen my house anywhere, have you?"

"Your house?" said Christopher Robin.

"It gets very cold on my side of the forest," explained Eeyore. "So I built myself a little house to keep warm in, and I went back there this morning, and IT'S GONE!"

"Oh, Eeyore," said Christopher Robin.

Eeyore and Christopher Robin set off together to look for Eeyore's little house.

"There!" said Eeyore, "You see. Not a stick of it left!"

But Christopher Robin wasn't listening. In the distance he could hear ... what was it?

Christopher Robin moved closer to where the strange sound was coming from. It sounded like two voices singing—first a gruff one and then a higher, squeakier one.

"It's Pooh and Piglet!" said Christopher Robin.

Sure enough, there were Pooh and Piglet coming toward them.

"There's Christopher Robin!" squeaked Piglet.

"He's over by the place where we found all those sticks!"

After Christopher Robin had given Pooh a hug, he told Pooh and Piglet about the sad story of Eeyore's lost house. And the more he talked, the more Pooh and Piglet's eyes seemed to get bigger and bigger.

"The fact is . . ." said Pooh. "Well, the fact is . . ."

"It's like this," said Piglet ". . . only WARMER."

"What's warmer?" asked Christopher Robin.

"The other side of the wood, where Eeyore's house is," said Piglet. "We'll show you," said Pooh.

So they went over to the other side of the forest, and sure enough there was Eeyore's house.

"It IS my house," said Eeyore. "And I built it where I said I did. The wind must have blown it here." And Eeyore happily settled down in his new house.

Pooh, Piglet and Christopher Robin went back home to lunch, and on the way Pooh and Piglet told him about the Awful Mistake they had made. Christopher Robin just laughed, and they all sang Pooh's song all the way home.

Tiddley Pom! Tiddley Pom!

Enjoy another wintry tale
with Winnie-the-Pooh and friends!

ISBN 978 1 4052 7938 3